The Ghost
on Main Street

The Ghost
on Main Street

by Warren Hussey Bouton

Illustrated by Barbara Kauffmann Locke

Hither Creek Press
Short Hills, New Jersey

*This book is dedicated to
loved ones past and present...
with special thanks to my
family and friends who have
helped make a dream
become a reality.*

CHAPTER 1

The screen door burst open with a crash as Ben and I ran into the kitchen, screaming "Hi Grandma!" We threw our arms around our grandmother as she wiped her doughy hands on her apron.

"What're you making?" Ben blurted as he noticed the bowl half-filled with what seemed to have the potential for chocolate chip cookies.

"What do you think?" Grandma replied. "Can't you smell them, or has a year's worth of growing ruined your nose for the smell of baking cookies?"

"For heaven's sake, isn't it always the

way?" Grandpa muttered as he squeezed through the kitchen door loaded down with enough suitcases and backpacks to supply our every need for the weeks to come. "Everybody else stands around gabbing while I do all the work."

Ben and I knew when Grandpa was teasing and when he wasn't, and by the look in his eye this was definitely one of those times we needed to help in a hurry.

I couldn't believe we were really here. This was the second summer our parents had sent us to Nantucket by ourselves to visit our grandparents. Nantucket was a great place to spend the summer, especially if you liked the beach. Thirty miles at sea off the coast of Massachusetts, Nantucket has miles and miles of sand, surf, and fun in the sun! There are all kinds of places to ride bikes and the town is like something out of a picture postcard, with beautiful old mansions and huge trees along the cobblestoned Main Street.

Grandma and Grandpa's place was an ancient two-story gray-shingled house. It had been in the family for generations and had always felt just a little spooky to me. The summer before, I had discovered that there was a very good reason for my fears. It wasn't just the old furniture and the portraits of all my dead ancestors hanging around, or even the damp, musty smell of wood that never seemed to dry out because of the fog. It wasn't just that the house creaked at night or had a long upstairs hallway with so many nooks and crannies that you could never be sure where the strange sounds were coming from. The house was scary because, as Ben and I had discovered, it was haunted!

"Sarah and Ben, you take your things upstairs," said Grandma. "Grandpa finally finished painting and papering the two front bedrooms, so you don't have to stay in the room next to the attic. I still don't understand why that room frightens you so much! Anyway, Sarah—you take the first one down the hall from the top of the stairs and Ben—you'll be in the next one down. Once you settle in, get yourselves cleaned up for dinner!" With that, Ben and I grabbed our things and headed for the stairs. I was sooooo thankful that I didn't have to stay in that back bedroom again! Our scary discovery last year had started in that back room.

After we had unpacked, Ben called from his room down the hall. "Sarah, let's go and check out the attic! Maybe we can find a ghost or two again! It might be fun…"

"Ben—knock it off!" I shouted. "There aren't going to be any ghosts, goblins, or ghouls this year."

If only I had been right. I didn't know it yet, but my brother and I were about to start a new and scary adventure!

CHAPTER
2

Dinnertime with Grandma and Grandpa was always an event. Not only was Grandma one of the best cooks on the island, but there was plenty of lively conversation to go along with the wonderful food. Tonight we feasted on spaghetti and the best garlic bread you ever tasted. Ben was full of stories of his baseball triumphs, from the six scoreless innings he'd pitched in a Little League playoff game to the time when he was a catcher and threw two runners out in one game. Grandma caught us up on the changes around the island and Grandpa grumbled about all the work he'd been doing around the house. Whenever I got a chance to squeeze into the conversation I shared stories of my singing and acting in the latest musical at school.

When dinner was over and the dishes were cleared, washed, and put away we all moved into the living room. Ben and Grandpa started a game of checkers. Of course, before Ben knew what was happening Grandpa was beating him and my dear little brother was whining like crazy. Grandma and I spent the time enjoying each other's company until I looked up and noticed a strange picture on the wall. I'm sure it had been there forever, but I guess I just never really saw it before. It was an old picture of a teenage boy who looked very sad. "Who's that, Grandma?" I asked. "Why is he so sad?"

Looking up, Grandma said, "Oh, that's Cyrus, one of your ancestors. His family lived in this house back in the 1800's. That picture was painted shortly before he died."

"Why did he die, Grandma?" I wondered aloud.

"They say he died of a broken heart. Cyrus was a seaman on a whaling ship. While he was out on one of those three-year trips to the Pacific, the girl he loved was killed in the Great Fire of Nantucket. That was sometime in the mid 1800's. When his ship returned and Cyrus learned that she was gone, he never left this house again... alive."

The night wore on. Ben was trounced at checkers time and again by Grandpa. Ben just never knew when enough was enough. Grandma kept knitting and I tried to read, but I just couldn't get young Cyrus out of my head. He looked so unhappy! Even after I went to bed his sad eyes haunted me. I wondered if the room I was staying in had been his. After a long time I began to drift peacefully off to sleep, but suddenly, I heard something. It sounded like footsteps out in the hallway. I just knew it was my annoying brother trying to scare me. I turned on my light and shouted "Okay, Ben, you can stop now. I know it's you and you want me to scream and carry on—but it's not going to work tonight. I've lived with you long enough to know that you're trying to scare me!" Ben usually started to laugh as soon as I caught him at one his tricks. But there was no answer, and the footsteps came closer and closer to my door and then stopped. Quickly, I jumped out of bed and ran to try to catch Ben as I opened the door...but no one was there! The hall was empty. There was nothing but shadows and my own fears.

Closing my bedroom door behind me, I slowly moved back to my bed. I knew I had heard someone out there. If it wasn't Ben, who could it be? I turned off my light and as I settled back into bed I began to feel a gentle, sad presence in the darkness. I tried to pretend that it was just my imagination, but it felt so real. As I lay there, I remembered Cyrus again. I couldn't get him out of my head. It was spooky. And it wasn't the last time that I felt something spooky on this trip.

CHAPTER 3

The next morning as I ate a fantastic breakfast of scrambled eggs and homemade sticky-buns, I told Grandma that I had spent a lot of time last night thinking about poor Cyrus. "Grandma, when did you say the Great Fire was?"

"I'm not really sure," Grandma answered. "But I'll bet anything it's in one of those Nantucket history books I have in the den. While you finish eating, let me just go and check. If you're so interested, the least I can do is take a quick look for you."

A few minutes later Grandma called out

to me as she moved across the dining room. "Sure enough, here it is!" She walked into the kitchen reading from a big book. "It was in 1846. As a matter of fact, in two days, July 13th, it's the anniversary of that fire. How about that?"

How about that was right! I couldn't believe that the footsteps in the hall, the presence in my room, and the anniversary of the Great Fire—not to mention the death of Cyrus' true love—were all a coincidence! What was going on? My terror and fears from last summer started to swell up inside me again! It couldn't be happening—not two summers in a row!

Suddenly, Grandma broke the spell. "It's going to be a beautiful day. Why don't you get your lazy brother out of bed so he can have some breakfast before I shut down this restaurant of mine, and while he's savoring my sticky buns you can get ready for the beach. Grandpa will drop you off at the Jetties as soon as everybody is ready and I'll pack you a lunch."

During the ride to the beach in Grandpa's truck, Ben chattered away, still licking the sticky-bun frosting from his fingers. Grandpa's dog Rusty sat on a little shelf behind the seat so he could look out the window. I was in the back of the truck for the trip because I didn't feel like talking to anybody. I needed to think. Was the presence in my room last night really Cyrus? What did he want? How many ghosts did that old house have anyway? Why me? Why come to see me after all these years? I couldn't get any of it out of my head. I certainly wasn't looking forward to another night in that room.

CHAPTER
4

It was a great day for the beach. There was hardly a cloud in the sky and a gentle breeze was coming in off the water. Jetties Beach was crowded as always. Lots of families went there because there was a playground for the little kids when they got bored with the beach. There was also a place where you could rent windsurfers and sunfish

It was low tide, and Ben and I wandered the beach for a while until we found a good spot to dump our stuff. Grandma had, as always, loaded us down with beach towels, sunscreen, and a couple of little coolers to keep our lunches cold. The spot where we finally put our things was right next to the Jetties. The giant rocks seemed to stretch out into the ocean forever, forming a long wall of stone to protect the entrance to the harbor, especially when the water was whipped up by a storm. On great days like this it was fun to see how far out you could walk on the rocks, and that's exactly what we did. As we jumped from stone to stone I looked out at the boats coming into and leaving the harbor. A beautiful two-masted schooner in full sail caught my eye. While I watched it I began to think of Cyrus and his whaling ship.

"Ben, what do you think it was like to sail off for three or four years on a ship not much bigger than that one?" I asked.

"You've got me! I don't think it would be much fun," Ben responded. "They probably stopped at some pretty neat places all over the world. But somehow I don't think it would be that great to be out on the open ocean without seeing land for weeks and weeks. I sure wouldn't want to climb up on those masts, especially during a storm. No fun! No fun at all."

"I agree, and I couldn't stand the idea of going out to kill whales," I said. "They're so big and beautiful. They're smart, too, with personalities and families. It must have been horrible to see them killed and boiled down for their oil and whalebone."

Ben added, "Yeah, it must have smelled pretty bad, too! What got you thinking about whaling?"

"That boy in the painting, Cyrus. Remember, Grandma said he was a sailor on a whaling ship." Then I hesitated. I wasn't sure I should say what was about to come out of my mouth but I just couldn't hold it in. "I think his ghost is still in that house."

"Come on, Sarah! Not again!" Ben was totally annoyed with me and his disgusted look showed it. "I know we were scared to death last summer and there was good reason for that. But how many ghosts can one house have? I think you're just making all this up to tease me. And that's *my* job! I'm the one who's supposed to drive *you* crazy remember? Now knock it off!"

I looked my brother right in the eye and I yelled, "It's true, Ben! Last night I heard footsteps in the hall. I opened the door and nobody, I mean *nobody*, was there! And when I got back into bed somebody was in my room. I couldn't see him. I couldn't hear him, but I felt him! I know it was the ghost of that boy in the picture. I'll bet you anything that the room I'm staying in was his room. And besides that, his girlfriend was killed in a fire. In just two days it will be the exact anniversary of that day. Something spooky is going on again, and whether we like it or not we're involved!"

"What do you mean 'we'?" Ben yelled angrily. "I haven't seen any ghost! Your buddy Cyrus didn't come and see me! Sounds like you're on your own with this one and that's just fine with me."

He turned and started running across the rocks to our towels. I looked out at the schooner again and wondered what the next days were going to bring. I had a feeling I wasn't going to like it, and unfortunately, I was right.

CHAPTER 5

The rest of the day, Ben and I didn't talk very much. Even through dinner we just sat on opposite sides of the table and listened to Grandma talk about what she had done all day. Grandpa sputtered and muttered about how hard he had worked mowing the lawn and how "other people had just sat around at the beach all day enjoying the sun and the sand!" I knew he was teasing, but not even his kidding brought a smile to either of our faces.

When it was time to go to bed we trudged up the stairs without a word to each other. I dreaded the idea of closing my eyes and trying to sleep in that room again. After brushing my teeth and changing into my pajamas, I reluctantly turned out my light. The room was quiet, but I didn't feel anything strange…yet. I was just starting to relax when I heard it. Someone was walking in the hall. Each step came closer and closer to my room. The floor creaked with every step. I wanted to pull the covers up over my head, but I didn't dare. What if it came into my room again? The footsteps finally stopped right in front of my door. The knob started to twist slowly. Suddenly, the door flew open and Ben came screaming into the room. "Look out! The ghost of Cyrus the sailor is going to get you!" he shouted. I jumped out of bed and wrapped my arm around his neck! "I'm going to clobber you, whether you're my brother or not!" We both fell to the floor. As we struggled, Ben started laughing. "What's the matter Sarah? Don't you have a sense of humor?"

I almost started laughing myself... but then I saw something pass by my open door. As quickly as I could, I let go of Ben and scrambled to look down the hall.

"What's the matter, Sarah? What did you see?"

"I don't know, but it was white, a little bit bigger than me, and it was moving toward the stairs!"

My brother ducked behind me as a ghostly white face appeared around the corner of the hallway. It was the face of the boy in the painting! It was Cyrus! When he saw us looking at him, he moved down the hall.

"Come on, Ben," I whispered.

"Are you nuts? That's a *ghost*! I'm not chasing after any ghost, whether he's one of my ancestors or not! Dead is dead, and he's up to no good!"

I grabbed Ben's arm and said, "You're coming with me, wimp!"

When we got to the head of the stairs, Cyrus was standing at the bottom looking up at us as if he were waiting. Then, as clear as day, he said in a sad voice, "Help me...Help me." Then he moved off again.

"What did he say?" Ben whispered.

"He said 'Help me.' Come on, how dangerous can a ghost be if he needs our help? Let's go." I started down the stairway with Ben slinking behind. Just when we reached the bottom we saw Cyrus duck around the corner and straight through a door. He just went right through it...and was gone.

"What's on the other side of that door, Sarah?" Ben whispered in a shaky voice.

"It's the cellar," I said as I lifted the latch

and looked down into the darkness.

"I'm not going down there," Ben groaned.

I could tell he was right on the edge of total terror, and so was I, so I gave in. "Okay, Ben. We won't go down tonight. Maybe we can check out the cellar tomorrow in the daylight."

But as we looked into the shadows and darkness that was the cellar, Cyrus' voice came to us again. It was slow, desperate, and pleading. "Help me...Please help me...Save Abigail..."

Ben slammed the cellar door and ran up the stairs. But I couldn't leave Cyrus like that. I opened the door just a crack and whispered, "I'll help you, Cyrus. Not tonight, but tomorrow. Don't worry, I'll help save Abigail."

I just hoped I'd know how.

CHAPTER 6

I had a hard time getting to sleep that night. I tossed and turned in my bed for hours wondering what I could do to help our new-found friend, Cyrus. I could tell that Ben was having a hard time sleeping too, because throughout the night I heard him tossing and turning in his room.

Grandma was pretty talkative at breakfast. She went on and on about the family history and how our ancestors had been one of the first twelve families to settle on the island. Another of our ancestors had been the captain of the first ship from Nantucket to catch a sperm whale. That single event began the transformation of Nantucket from a quiet fishing village to the whaling capital of the world. Of course, I didn't tell Grandma how I felt about the whole whaling thing, but whenever she talked about it, my skin started to crawl.

Ben was very quiet during breakfast. I could tell that he was still terrified by what we had seen last night. Finally, when we had devoured our breakfast of french toast with real Vermont maple syrup, he said, "Grandma, is there anything you need from the store? Sarah and I were thinking about walking downtown this morning."

I looked at Ben with total surprise. We hadn't talked about going to town at all. But I knew my brother well enough to realize that it was his way of telling me that we needed to talk. "How about it, Grandma," I said, "can we pick up some fresh tomatoes from the vegetable truck or maybe stop in at the Hub and pick up Grandpa's newspaper?" The Hub was like a big newspaper stand where you could buy newspapers and magazines from all over the world. It was one of our regular stops when we were visiting, because we were always running out of stuff to read.

"That would be nice, kids," Grandma answered. She got her purse so she could give us money for her errands. "Since you're going that way, would you drop these letters off at the post office? And would you pick up some tomatoes, a cucumber or two if they look good, and a *Cape Cod Times* from the Hub for Grandpa? That would be a big help."

Soon Ben and I were making our way down Main Street. "What's this all about Ben?" I asked as we passed the huge old houses and the massive elm trees that line the sidewalks on the way to town.

"I just had to get out of that house," Ben answered. "Sarah, I had enough of ghosts last year. This is really scary! I don't care if you think Cyrus is friendly, sad, or lonely. It's not my fault his girlfriend was killed in a fire. It's spooky! I don't want to have anything to do with ghosts. It just means trouble."

"I'm not wild about it either, Ben, but we don't have any choice! For some reason Cyrus has picked us, or at least me, and I need your help. I don't know what I can do for someone who died over 150 years ago. But I don't think Cyrus is going to leave us alone just because we don't want to help!"

Ben didn't say anything for a long time. We had finished all of our errands and were just starting to head home when suddenly he whispered in surprise, "There he is!"

I looked up the street and didn't see anybody I thought we knew. "What are you talking about Ben? Who did you see?"

Ben was as white as a sheet. He had stopped dead in his tracks and was just staring up the street. "It's Cyrus!" he muttered.

When I looked again there he was, plain as day, standing on the corner of Centre Street. Everyone else was walking right by him, so it was pretty clear that we were the only ones who could see our ghostly friend.

Once Cyrus knew we had seen him, he scooted around the corner. We followed him past the fancy gift shops and clothing stores. He looked back from time to time to make sure we were still there. Finally, he stopped right in front of a restaurant. Trying to be funny, Ben said, "Gee, maybe he's hungry!" But Cyrus turned toward us and he wasn't laughing. He stared straight into our eyes, pointed at the building, and pleaded, "Help me... Save Abigail. You have to help me..." And then he was gone.

CHAPTER
7

That night after dinner, as Ben was trying once again to win a game of checkers against Grandpa, and Grandma and I were cleaning up in the kitchen, I finally worked up the nerve to ask, "Grandma, have you ever noticed anything strange around this house? I mean, you haven't run into any ghosts...have you?"

"Oh for heaven's sake, not you too! Every once in a while when we have company, somebody asks that silly question. I don't know what it is that spooks people so much about this house. I guess it's just because the place is so old and so many generations of our family have lived here that people think it's haunted. Sure, the house creaks and moans every so often, but it's just an old house showing its age and adjusting to the weather. Wood expands and contracts with the heat, the cold, and the moisture of the fog, that's all. There's no such thing as ghosts. At least I've never met one!"

"But what about Cyrus, Grandma? Have you ever seen him?"

"Oh come on now, Sarah! Of course I haven't seen him, except in the painting. He's been dead for years and years. How am I supposed to see him?"

I didn't know what to say. Now, after everything she'd said, I wasn't going to tell Grandma I'd seen a ghost. She would think I had lost my mind! "Can you tell me anything about him or about his girlfriend?" I asked.

"Not much to tell. I already told you he died of a broken heart. The anniversary of the Great Fire is tomorrow—it started somehow, they say in a hat shop down on Main Street about where the coffee shop is now. For some reason, the fire brigades in town didn't get things under control very quickly. The fire spread from building to building until it had worked its way up to the top of Main Street. Then the wind shifted and it moved down Centre Street to what is now the Jared Coffin House. Then the wind changed again and the fire burned all the way to the harbor. It devastated the downtown area, and of course in the process the love of Cyrus' life died in one of the houses. The way the fire burned, I don't know if anyone could have saved her even if they had wanted to."

That wasn't what I wanted to hear. Cyrus needed us to save Abigail. I didn't know what we could do. I didn't know how we could stop something that had happened so long ago. But I did know that if there was any chance, Cyrus would make sure we took it.

I didn't have much longer to wait before Cyrus made us a part of Nantucket's history!

CHAPTER
8

The footsteps in the hallway came just as I was turning my light out for the night. This time I was ready. On our way home after meeting Cyrus in town, Ben and I had decided we would go to bed at the regular time, but we wouldn't change into our pajamas. That way we'd be ready to follow Cyrus if he came. Well, he came all right, and it sounded as if he was right outside my door.

I heard Ben in the hall calling to me, "Sarah, he's here... You'd better still be awake because I'm not chasing after any ghost by myself!"

I thought about making Ben sweat a little, but I had to see Cyrus for myself. I wasn't disappointed. There he was, standing in the hall as if he was waiting for me.

"Help me. Save Abigail," he said, and then started moving down the hall to the stairs again.

"This is it, Ben. Are you up for it? If we follow him tonight we're committing ourselves to helping him."

"But how can we help a ghost? Whatever happened was a long time ago, and here we are more than 150 years later. It's stupid! I just don't get it."

"Ben, you're either in or out. Stay here if you're chicken, but I'm going!"

By the time I made it to the bottom of the stairway, Cyrus was nowhere to be seen. Much to my surprise, Ben showed up behind me. He said, "Okay, Sarah you win. I wouldn't want you to have all the fun. Besides, if I'm not along to protect you, who knows what kind of trouble you'll be in!"

I wanted to smack him in the head, but instead I made my way over to the cellar door on a hunch that Cyrus had taken the same path as the night before. Sure enough, our sad ghost was standing there waiting for us. He waved his hand to call us down.

"There must be a light switch here somewhere," I said, fumbling along the wall until I finally found it.

The stairs groaned as we made our way down. The whole place smelled of sawdust and paint from all Grandpa's projects. By the time our feet had touched the cellar floor, Cyrus was on the other side of the basement, going out an old door that led to the driveway.

"Where's he going now?" Ben sputtered. "He doesn't need to open that door. He's a *ghost*. He can go right through it if he really wants to."

Cyrus turned and motioned to us again. "Come," he whispered. "Save Abigail."

We crept across the cellar. Ben was so close to me that it felt as if we were glued together when we stepped through the door.

Then, without warning, there was an incredible flash of light that blinded both of us. We fell onto the driveway just as the cellar door slammed shut. Ben and I struggled to open it, but the door was locked. Cyrus was nowhere to be seen, but from the other side of the door we heard his haunting voice one last time.

"Go... save... Abigail."

We looked around, then at each other, and we knew that our adventure had begun!

CHAPTER
9

"Where on earth did you get those clothes?" I laughed as I caught a good look at Ben in the shimmering light of the full moon. I couldn't believe my eyes. He was wearing knickers! You know, the old-fashioned pants that stop just below the knees. He also had on stockings and shoes that looked as if they belonged in a museum. His shirt had long sleeves that billowed out around his wrists. "Ooh, Ben, I like your little cap! What were you doing tonight, going through Grandma's trunks of antique clothes?"

Ben snickered right back, "Well if you

think I look funny, you should get a peek at yourself!" I glanced down and just about fainted. I was wearing a long dress with lace and the most bizarre apron I'd ever seen in my life. "What's going on here? These clothes look like something out of the..."

"The 1850's?" Ben whispered.

As soon as he said that, I knew he was right. Of course, the fact that a horse and buggy was trotting along Main Street in the glow of gas streetlights helped the reality of our situation sink in too!

"What happened? How in the world did we end up here?" I wondered aloud.

Ben was batting a thousand when he answered, "It was Cyrus. He led us through the cellar door and somehow we stepped back in time. I don't know how he did it. But I don't know why we were following a ghost through the house either! This is all your fault! You and your stupid 'We have to help poor Cyrus!' Well, *now* what are we going to do?"

"Don't panic, Ben," I yelled just a little too loudly and with a bit more fear than I wanted to show my brother. "Maybe we haven't really gone back in time. Maybe Cyrus is just playing a trick on us. If we can't get back into the house through the cellar door, let's go around to the kitchen and see if we can find Grandma and Grandpa. Maybe they can help us figure out what's going on."

We ran around to the back of the house as fast as we could in the strange shoes and clothes. I tripped a couple of times on the hem of my long dress. Ben and I were both relieved to find the back door unlocked, with a light shining in the kitchen. We banged through the door and then we stopped in our tracks. Everything in the room was different, and right in the middle of the kitchen there was a huge man in a nightshirt that reached down to the floor. He was carrying a candle and seemed as surprised to see us as we were to see him.

"Who in the world are you?" he bellowed. "What do you think you're doing, walking into my house in the middle of the night? He looked very angry, and moved toward us. "Get out of this house—right now!"

He didn't need to say it twice. We were out the door and running for our lives!

We ran as fast as we could through the back yards of the neighborhood. We finally came to a wooden fence too high to climb, but as we inched along clinging to the shadows we found a loose board that Ben and I could just squeeze through. Much to our surprise, we found ourselves standing and staring at a building we knew as the Old Gaol...except it wasn't old!

"Let's get out of here!" Ben shrieked

when he realized where we were. "This is where we'll end up if that man in Grandma and Grandpa's house has his way!"

"Shut up and hide behind those bushes," I muttered as I pushed him toward a corner of the jailyard that was overgrown with bushes and small, scruffy oak trees. "This is the last place they'll ever look for us!"

When we had caught the breath that we had lost from running so hard, Ben looked at me and with a trace of a whimper in his voice asked, "What are we going to do?"

"Ben, I don't know, and we're not going to find out anything more tonight. No telling who may be looking for us now. Let's try and rest a bit. I'll stay awake and when it's almost dawn we'll go back through the fence and head downtown. Maybe then we'll be able to figure out what's going on."

While Ben settled down I couldn't help but worry and wonder what we'd have to do to get back to Grandma and Grandpa's house. Well, getting back to the house was no problem, really. Getting back to our own *time—that* was the problem!

CHAPTER
10

"Ben, wake up. We need to move!" I nudged my little brother with my elbow as the eastern sky started to brighten. "We'd better get out of here before somebody finds us and makes us permanent guests!"

Slowly moving along the fence, we managed to find the loose board that was our door to the outside world, and each of us squeezed through.

"Okay, I think Main Street is over that way. Try to stay low, just in case somebody is awake and looking out their windows. Once we hit the street we'll just look like two kids on the way to town."

When our feet touched the sidewalk of Main Street, both of us relaxed a lot! But as we looked around there was no doubt in either of our minds that things were different. There were no cars parked on the street and no electric lights. We could see oil lamps or candles burning in a few houses and every once in a while we heard horses whinny from the back yards. One thing was for sure, we weren't in our own time any more! The chances of seeing a Jeep, a minivan, or a motor scooter were zero!

We were almost in the heart of town when we heard a man shouting. It was the town crier calling at the top of his lungs. His words sent a shiver through our bones because he instantly confirmed our very worst fears. "Six o'clock and all is well. Rise and shine. It's time to greet the new day, July 13th, in the year of our Lord 1846!"

"1846!!" Ben groaned as he rolled his eyes. "What have you gotten me into? 'Let's follow Cyrus! Don't be a chicken! Let's help him! He's so sad!' Well, look at where helping that stupid ghost has gotten us! We've been chased by an angry man. We spent the night in a corner of a jailyard, and now we find out that sure enough we've traveled back in time to 1846. If you ask me, that's a problem!"

I couldn't take it any more! I sat down in the middle of the sidewalk, covered my face with my hands, and started to cry. Ben looked at me and knew that he'd gone too far. He put his hand on my shoulder. "Come on, Sarah, I didn't mean it! We'll figure a way out of this. At least, get out of the middle of the sidewalk! Sooner or later somebody's going to come along and it would be better if we didn't attract a lot of attention."

I knew he was right, but I was so tired. Too many things had happened through the night and I just couldn't make sense of it all. I moved over to the curb of the street and sat for a long time, my feet resting on the cobblestones. My sobs finally turned to whimpers, and then the tears started to dry at last. "I don't know why Cyrus would do this to us. I never thought helping him would take us back in time. What can we do here?"

Then it came to me! "Ben, what did the town crier yell a minute ago? What was the date?"

"He said it was July 13, 1846."

"That's it, Ben! Grandma said the Great

Fire was on July 13, 1846. It's *tonight*! Cyrus wants us to save Abigail! We have to find her house and somehow protect her from the fire. That's why we're here! Remember, he kept saying, 'Help me. Save Abigail.' That's what he wants us to do. The real Cyrus, the alive Cyrus is off on a whaling ship and we're supposed to save her so that when he gets back she'll be alive and waiting for him. But how can we do that?"

Ben exclaimed, "I know! We'll find the house Cyrus pointed out. It was on Centre Street. We can find it, I'm sure we can. It was on a corner... you know, where that restaurant is...was...will be...oh, you know what I mean! I know we can find it. The house may look different, but we'll find it. We have to!"

CHAPTER
11

"There it is!" Abigail's house was right where we thought it would be. It really wasn't so hard to find our way around the old Nantucket. We stood across the street and gazed at the simple home. It was like so many other houses on the island, with two stories, plain gray shingles, and wooden shutters. But somehow, knowing it was going to burn that night made Ben and me feel weird. Staring at the house, we lost track of time until a booming voice came from behind us.

"So, my good children, what do we find so interesting this early in the morning? I trust you *are* good children!" We were almost startled out of our skin to turn and find a big, burly policeman looking at us with suspicion in his eyes.

"Oh yes... sir. We were just... uh... waiting... to see Abigail," I managed to stutter. "We're to spend the day with Abigail. She lives right over there, and we were so excited to see her that we seem to have gotten up too early. I think we should be off for a while and then come back. It doesn't seem as if anyone is up yet."

"I don't think I recognize either of you two," the policeman said. "What're your names, might I ask, and where are you from?"

We had to think quick! If we used our own last name he'd know we weren't from the island. But what was an old Nantucket name? I

panicked until I caught sight of a street sign just a stone's throw from where we were standing. "Hussey," I blurted. We're Sarah and Benjamin Hussey. My brother and I are visiting our grandparents here and we just met Abigail yesterday. We'll be going now, sir."

Yes, you be off, young children," the man said. "Perhaps you'll see Abigail a little later. But if I find you standing around and staring as if you're about to cause mischief, you'll be seeing me again!"

Ben and I hurried away, thanking our lucky stars for a well-placed street sign.

"What are we going to do, Sarah? We have to see if we can get back to find Abigail."

Muttering softly I said, "I know, Ben! But right now that guy doesn't want us standing around staring at her house. We'll leave for a while and then come back. Let's keep moving and try to stay away from the cops!"

"Can we try to find some food," said Ben. "I'm getting real hungry."

"I am too but that may be easier said than done. Let's head down to the docks and see if we can find something to eat there. With all the ships coming and going, there's bound to be plenty of people, and where there are people, there might be food. Nantucket was the whaling capital of the world in the 1800's. I may not like whaling, but this is a once-in-a-lifetime chance to see history up close…real close!"

CHAPTER 12

Ben and I had read about Nantucket and the number of whaling ships that had called the island home. Grandma had made us! But nothing prepared us for how lively the docks were that morning. People were coming and going, loading and unloading, carrying harpoons, food, ropes, and rolling huge barrels to and from all the ships that were tied up at the docks.

We tried to blend in, moving along with all the workmen as they went about their jobs.

"Sarah, I'm hungry!" Ben complained again.

"I know! I feel the same way, but what am I supposed to do about it? We don't have any money, so keep your eyes open. Maybe we'll find something if we're lucky."

It was incredible to see a 19th century seaport in action. The sights, sounds, and smells were overwhelming. Time seemed to fly, and for a while Ben even forgot how hungry he was!

Finally, as we were standing beside what looked like the biggest ship in the harbor, we spotted a man carrying three big wooden boxes toward the gangplank. They were awkward and heavy, and as we watched he slipped on the wet wharf. His feet went out from under him, and the boxes flew into the air. They landed with a crash, and one broke open. It was filled with large wafers of hardtack, an important part of the food supplies for sailors on their whaling trips. Hardtack is tough, and not very tasty—Grandma had made some for us once—but it is food, and we were hungry! And here it was, spread in many broken pieces all over the dock around this poor man, who was swearing like the sailor he was.

"You want food, Ben," I said. "This is our chance! For every two pieces you pick up, make sure one goes into your pocket!" That's all I needed to say, and before the sailor knew what was happening he had two of the most helpful children on the island working at his side. It didn't take long before he was on his way back up the gangplank and Ben and I were walking down the dock with pockets full of hardtack.

"Let's try to find a place where we can just sit, think and eat." I said to Ben. "We can go just beyond the wharves, back toward the main part of town and maybe sit on the steps of a boardinghouse I noticed there. It must be where the sailors stay when they're in port. No one will mind if we rest there for a bit. It's pretty rough and noisy on the docks."

We found a place to sit. Once we started to piece together the Nantucket we knew with the Nantucket we were experiencing now, we felt a little bit better. For a few minutes we sat and talked about our strange adventure. We looked up toward the town, which was just coming to life, and then stared out at the harbor, with all those old-fashioned sailing ships. It was beautiful, exciting and scary all at once. Then we dug into our pockets and feasted on the bland biscuits. It was our first meal since Cyrus had led us through the cellar door.

CHAPTER
13

"So what do we do now, Sarah?" Ben asked when we'd finished our tasteless but filling feast of hardtack.

"We wait. Then we head back to Centre Street and try to find Abigail. The Great Fire is going to start sometime before midnight tonight. Grandma said the first building to catch fire was a hat shop on Main Street. Once it's going, the fire will move up Main Street near the bank and then down toward Abigail's house. Finally, it'll head for the harbor. We have to get to Abigail before her house burns and then head west. The fire won't go that way."

Before I could go on, Ben jumped in and asked, "But once we save her, what do we do with her?"

"I haven't thought of that yet! Maybe we take her back to Grandma and Grandpa's house. Cyrus knew her. He loved her! His parents will know what to do with her. That must have been Cyrus' father who chased us out of the kitchen. Wherever we take her, we have to find Abigail and make sure she's safe, and that's all that matters!"

As the sun moved higher in the sky, the combination of the warmth and our full stomachs made both of us drift off to sleep. When we woke up, the wharves were still bustling and we could see that people in the center of town were going about their daily business.

"Just look at all those big whaling ships, Ben," I said. "When they sail out of Nantucket Harbor it's for three or four years. Can you imagine living on a ship all that time, without seeing or even hearing from your family and friends back home?"

"No, I can't," Ben said. "And Grandma says a lot of those men who went to sea never came back. Do you think any of them ever thought about not getting back home?"

It was time to be honest, and so I said, "I don't know, Ben. But I do!"

"Don't even think that way, Sarah! We've gotten out of tough spots before, and we'll get out of this one too."

"You're right... I'm sorry," I said. "Cyrus wouldn't have led us here unless we could pull it off. Together we can do it! I think it's time to go and look for Abigail again. The sun is moving toward the west, and we don't want to run out of time before it gets dark. We need to know what we're going to do before the fire starts."

CHAPTER
14

We made our way back to Centre Street, but as we got close to Abigail's house, we saw the same policeman we'd seen early in the morning! "Oh no!" I moaned. "If he spots us there may be more questions. Quick, Ben, under here!" I couldn't believe our luck. Right there beside us was an opening under some porch stairs. I shoved Ben down and as fast as I could scampered under the steps behind him.

"Do you think he saw us?" Ben whispered.

"No, but look through here. We can see

Abigail's house! This is a great spot to watch for her."

The afternoon sunlight was starting to fade when we finally noticed a girl just a little bit older than me walking down the street toward Abigail's house.

"I'll bet you anything that's Abigail!" I was so excited I could hardly control myself.

"But we have to know for sure," my brother butted in.

"I know that! I'm going to go talk with her. It's the only way." I sighed with nervousness. "Ready or not Abigail, here I come!"

I slipped out from under the stairs and brushed the dirt off my dress as I walked toward the girl. As we were about to pass each other I blurted, "Excuse me, is your name Abigail?"

She stopped short and looked at me with surprise. "Why, indeed I am! And who are you? I do not think I have ever seen you before."

"My name is Sarah... I'm a distant cousin

of someone you know. His name is Cyrus."

"Cyrus!" she blushed. "Of course I know Cyrus...we're...very good friends! Have you heard from him?" Abigail quickly looked around to see if anyone was watching and grabbed my arm, whispering, "Oh, I do want to hear all about him. Word has come that his ship is returning soon. Come to my room and tell me everything you know!"

Abigail dragged me after her. We slipped in the back door, stole quietly up the steep stairway and down the hall to her room. She plopped me on her bed and shut the door behind her. "Now—do tell me what you know about Cyrus! Please!"

At first I didn't know what to say. I stumbled and stammered until the words finally came to me. "He's worried about you. He's afraid you're in danger!"

"Oh, that is just like Cyrus!" She giggled. "He is always concerned about me, and from time to time he has...premonitions about the future. Most of the time it is silliness."

This was my chance to warn Abigail, and I had to take it. "He's worried about a fire, Abigail, a bad one...one that will wipe out most of the town!"

"That is foolish! We have wonderful fire brigades! They always answer the bell quickly and sometimes two or three teams of firemen from different parts of town all show up. They can put out a house fire in no time. A big fire could never happen here!"

Abigail's tone told me she thought this was foolishness, and that upset me. "Abigail, Cyrus wanted you to promise me that if you hear a fire bell you'll get away from this house as fast as you can! He knows what he's talking about, and if anything ever happens to you it will haunt him for the rest of his life! You have to promise or he'll never forgive himself. He'll never forgive *me*!"

"My goodness—all right! You *must* be related to Cyrus. You worry as much as he does! I promise…"

At that moment we heard her mother calling from downstairs, "Abigail, it is suppertime."

She jumped from the bed and grabbed my arm again, saying, "You must leave now. Mother mustn't see you. She doesn't like me talking to people she doesn't know."

Abigail ran down the backstairs as I snuck down the front, scampered out the door and made my way back to our hiding place.

"What happened?" Ben clamored. "What took you so long?"

"We talked, and I made her promise to leave the house if she heard the fire bell! I think she will... but I'm not really sure."

"Well, she'd better, if she knows what's good for her!" he said. "I'm hungry again! How about another gourmet hardtack meal?"

Slowly the sun began to set, and as night claimed the streets of Nantucket, Ben and I drifted off to sleep.

It was the last time we would know a moment's peace on this side of the cellar door.

CHAPTER
15

The frantic clanging of a bell woke Ben and me from our sleep. We looked out from our hiding place and saw people running past us toward Main Street.

"What's that?" Ben asked, rubbing his eyes.

"It must be the fire bell. It's started! The hat shop must be burning."

We scrambled out to the street and saw a faint glow over the rooftops to the south. The smell of smoke was drifting in the night breeze.

I looked over at Abigail's house. It was

completely dark. "We have to go into Abigail's and get her out of there!" I said.

"We've got plenty of time, Sarah. You said yourself things are just starting. I'm going to Main Street. I want to see this…"

I was now shouting at Ben's back as he ran toward the fire. "No, we're here to save…" But it was too late. He was off. I looked over at the house but I couldn't let Ben go off by himself. We had to stick together.

By the time we got to Main Street there were two fire brigades setting up in front of the hat shop. Smoke was pouring from the windows. But instead of putting out the fire, the two groups of firemen were yelling at each other, arguing over who should have the privilege of putting out the fire! Even as they screamed at each other, the wind began to pick up and embers from the hat shop blew across an alleyway and set fire to the roof of the building next door. Before the firemen knew it, there were two more stores ablaze. When they finally noticed what was happening, the screaming turned from anger to total panic. Now there was more than enough fire for both groups!

"Ben, this is starting to get out of hand," I said. "Those sparks are landing on more rooftops and the wind is feeding the flames. We *must* get back to Abigail's."

All of a sudden we heard an explosion! The firemen were using dynamite to blow up some of the buildings, hoping to create a fire break—an empty space that the fire couldn't jump across. They hoped this would keep the flames from spreading. The sound rocked the night. A woman stood on the front porch of the

Methodist Church, shouting that she wouldn't allow them to dynamite it. We watched in horror as store after store lit up, flames shooting into the air. Just before the fire made it to the church, the wind shifted, driving it in a new direction... toward Abigail's house.

"Ben, the fire has changed direction. We have to go... *now*!" I yanked on Ben's arm. "We have to save her, Ben. It's now or never! This way! Run!"

We ran as fast as we could down Federal Street, trying to beat the flames. I yelled to Ben over the roar of the fire and wind. "If we take a left on Chestnut Street that will take us right to her house."

"Yeah, but if the fire shifts again before we get there, Sarah, we're toast!"

"It won't if we runnnnn!"

We could see the flames moving up
Centre Street. The air was filled with embers,
and the heat of the fire was now creating its own

draft. We could feel the heat as we ran. Sparks landed on our clothes and we had to keep slapping them out so they didn't burn us. The smoke was so thick we could hardly breathe.

We reached Abigail's house just ahead of the fire. I crashed through the back door with Ben right behind me. Screaming at the top of our lungs, we frantically scrambled up the back stairs, searching for Abigail's room. Smoke filled the house and I heard someone coughing down the hall. I threw open a bedroom door and there she was, crouched in the corner of her room and looking terrified. Ben and I grabbed her as the curtains in the window burst into flames from a flying ember.

"The front steps," I yelled. Coughing all the way, we bolted down the stairs and through the front door. The street was in total chaos.

People were running in every direction. The sound of the flames and wind were frightening. Giant elm trees were turning into enormous torches blazing up into the sky.

"Ben!" I shouted, "Hussey Street! We need to get to Hussey Street. It's right over there!" With Abigail between us, we fought through the panicked crowd. It looked as if the entire island was on fire. At last, we made it to Hussey Street, but just when we thought we were going to be safe, Ben tripped. Our momentum carried Abigail and me a few feet away and as we turned to help Ben a huge burning elm crashed down between us. For a minute I couldn't see my brother at all. I was terrified. Had he been crushed by the tree? I screamed, totally losing control. Before I knew what was happening, Abigail surged through the blazing branches. It seemed like forever, but only seconds later Abigail and Ben broke through the flames, running as fast as they could. There wasn't time to celebrate or even give them a hug. We ran and ran down the smoke-filled street, stumbling and coughing our way along until at last we were far enough away from the holocaust to feel safe. Panting for breath we collapsed in a pile.

We sat there exhausted for a long time. Finally, Abigail broke the silence. "You saved my life! You risked your own and you don't even know me! Why?"

"I told you before," I said. "Cyrus was worried about you. He asked us to help, that's all! You didn't have to go after Ben either, but you did."

"Well I'm glad she did!" Ben moaned as

he wiped soot from his forehead. "I'm *real* glad
she did!"

The three of us rested for a bit, and when
we felt we could move again we made our way

up Gardner Street and then onto upper Main. We were relieved to finally spot Grandma and Grandpa's house. Standing on the front porch was the man we had encountered in the kitchen and a woman. They held each other and looked scared as they watched the fire in the distance. Abigail ran to them and there were plenty of hugs and kisses.

By the time Abigail turned to introduce us, Ben and I were already out of sight and around the house. We reached the cellar door and desperately tried to open it. For a scary minute it wouldn't budge, but then I kicked it and yelled, "She's safe, Cyrus! For crying out loud, let us in!" On the next yank, the door flew open. Before Cyrus could change his mind, we rushed through the door and there was a sudden flash of light. When we opened our eyes, we found ourselves lying on the cellar floor even as Grandma was calling down the stairs!

CHAPTER 16

"Sarah and Ben, what in the world are you doing down there? Get up here and have some breakfast or the kitchen will close and you can just wait until lunchtime!"

"Be right there, Grandma," I called as we hurried up the stairs. I hoped my voice sounded normal.

"Why, look at you!" Grandma fumed. "What did you get into down there?"

Ben and I looked at each other. Even though we were back in the clothes we'd been wearing before we'd gone out through the cellar door, our faces and hands were covered in soot!

"Did you two get into that old coal bin? I've been after Grandpa for years to get rid of that dirty coal. You'd think by now, though, that the two of you would be old enough or smart enough to stay away from it! Get yourselves upstairs and wash up. I'll throw together some breakfast for you and then you can head off to the beach for the day."

After I had washed off the soot I came down the stairs and looked into the living room. I had to smile as I looked at the old painting on the wall. I heard Ben trotting down the stairs and I called to him. "Ben, take a look at this!"

He came into the room and I pointed to the picture. It was different. Now two people were in it. They were Cyrus and Abigail, looking into each other's eyes with happiness.

"Hey Grandma, what happened to the painting of Cyrus?"

"What do you mean what happened to it?" Grandma came into the living room wiping her hands on her apron. "That picture has been hanging there for years and years, since long before I was born. Those are your ancestors, Cyrus and Abigail. They lived here once. The story goes that they had one of those fairy-tale marriages."

"Yes, Grandma that's one thing we know!" Ben and I grinned at each other and said together, "We know they lived happily ever after!"

Look for
Warren Hussey Bouton's
first book

Sea Chest
in the Attic

For more information about
Hither Creek Press
or to contact the author
send your email to:
Hithercreekpress@aol.com